AF416099

Amish Friendly

Beverly Price

Published by Trellis Publishing, 2021.

This is a work of fiction. Similarities to real people, places, or events are entirely coincidental.

AMISH FRIENDLY

First edition. July 14, 2021.

Copyright © 2021 Beverly Price.

ISBN: 979-8224371990

Written by Beverly Price.

AMISH FRIENDLY
BEVERLY PRICE

AMISH SUNSET

Chapter I

Rain decorated the grassy fields of Lancaster County. The sky was a cloud grey, the sun remaining absent as the county mourned for the loss of William Bradshire, a carpenter that had been known throughout the county for his kindness and love towards the people around him.

Friends and family had gathered in the county's cemetery for William's funeral, one of the mourners being William's love, Mary Lee Warner. Out of everyone there, Mary was the most damaged from it. William's parents had passed on early in his life due to illnesses and the remaining family he had weren't as close. If anything, Mary was the only one there who truly was family to him.

As Bishop David spoke about his memories with William, Mary thought to herself how God could do such a thing, to take away an innocent being this early in his life. William was only in his mid-twenties, like Mary. He had so much to experience in his life, but it was stripped away from him so early due to the accident.

"If anyone has anything to say, speak now." Bishop David said, stepping back and letting anyone step forward to speak.

There was a long pause, silence being present as Mary thought to herself. Eventually, she took a step forward, standing in front of the casket as she let out a depressed sigh.

"William...had a beautiful soul," Mary said quietly, holding onto a wildflower, "a soul that I have yet to find in any other human being."

Everyone was watching her speak, seeing what Mary had in her hand and what she had to say about William being gone.

"I can't imagine not meeting him in my life...all the memories we've made together...all the laughter, the love...I'm going to miss it." Mary spoke as tears ran down her cheeks. "I don't know if I will find another William in my life."

Some of William's family members began to have tears fall too as they listened to Mary's words about their lost kin. Mary soon stepped back from the casket, having finished speaking on the behalf of William's death. Bishop David soon stepped forward again, wiping some tears from his own eyes.

"Thank you Mary...I will say, before I close in prayer, that it will be difficult to find another William in our lives." Bishop David said to Mary before opening his Bible.

Verses from the Bible were soon spoken out loud, everybody bowing their heads in prayer as Bishop David spoke. While everyone listened, Mary wasn't listening to the verses, in fact, she was in her own mind at this point.

"*Why God...why would you take William away from me?*" Mary thought to herself. "*William didn't even get half way into his life...why would you take him now?*"

As she struggled with the idea of William passing on, Bishop David finished reading the verses, quietly speaking the word *amen* as he closed his Bible, everybody soon leaving the scene of the funeral, letting the casket to be lowered into the grave. While the casket lowered, Mary was the only one present, witnessing her love's final presence on the surface of Earth.

In regards to funeral traditions of the Amish, flowers were not placed on the casket. For Mary though, traditions meant nothing to her in this occasion. She took the wildflower that she was holding in her hand and tossed it down into the undug grave, letting it land on the coffin before the gravediggers began to bury the coffin.

"I love you so much William." Mary said as the coffin soon disappeared from the soil piling on top. Tears continued to fall onto the soil as she left the site of the funeral.

Chapter II

Several years later...the county had returned back to its normal ways, except for Mary. Ever since William passed away, Mary wasn't her old self. Her old cheerful personality had passed on as well, leaving her a closed up, emotionless woman in her mid-twenties.

She tried to return back to a normal life by going to church, seeing if God might be able to help her find peace, but the more she went the church, the more she began to question God. At times, she would find herself being angry at God for taking William away this early in his life. Eventually, Mary stopped going to church, which brought the concern of Bishop David, leading him to go to Mary's home.

Her house was a little way from town, being near one of the farms. She lived in a large house that belonged to William and his parents. Now that William passed on, Mary now owned the house and lived in it by herself.

Bishop David knocked on the front door, waiting for it to be opened. It took a few knocks before the door finally opened, Mary standing there in a stone grey dress.

"Yes?" Mary quietly said, looking at him with her expressionless face.

"May I come in?" Bishop David asked softly, his expression being hopeful that she would accept his request.

Mary let out a quiet sigh before she nodded, stepping out of the way for Bishop David to come in.

"Thank you...Mary." He said, soon walking into her home, looking around.

Mary shut the door behind Bishop David, walking past him and sitting down on a chair in the living room, continuing what she was doing before he knocked. When Bishop David sat down across from her, he noticed that she was knitting a quilt.

"Oh...I see that you've been busy with making a quilt." Bishop David said, giving Mary a gentle smile.

"Quilts. I've been busy making quilts." She said quickly, pointing in the corner to a basket of several quilts.

Bishop David was surprised by the amount of quilts she had made. "That's quite the number of quilts Mary." He said with a small laugh after.

Mary raised her eyebrows as she continued to knit the quilt. "I've found that work is one of the few things that keeps me from thinking about the past." She said softly, not making eye contact with Bishop David.

"Oh...well...if that's what helps you find peace." He said quietly, rubbing the back of his neck before he finally decided to talk about why he wanted to talk to her. "Mary...I'm worried about you."

She heard Bishop David, stopping for a second before she continued knitting the quilt. "Why?" Mary questioned him.

"I'm concerned for you because you haven't been going to church for months." Bishop David finally said, looking at her with a worried expression. "You were always an avid church-goer when William..." He said before realizing what he said, stopping in mid-sentence.

Mary immediately looked up when Bishop David brought up William, her knitting ceasing before she let out a sigh of disbelief escape her lips. She set the quilt and knitting needle down. "Please, do not ever bring up William to me again when comparing me to then and now." Mary said, her voice trembling as she had grown an upset expression.

Bishop David had become silent as he listened to Mary finally speak to him.

"I'm no longer the Mary from then because of the events that happened, and if you want to visit me and tell me how I use to love church and that you're concerned with me not being there on Sundays, then don't even speak, you're wasting your breath." Mary said to him, her eyes staring into his intensely.

Bishop David heard everything she was saying before he let out a sigh of sympathy. "I'm sorry Mary that you're like this...I didn't come here today to chastise you about not attending church. I came here because

I'm really concerned for what you've become. I want happiness for you, I want you to have that cheerful personality that everybody knew you for." He said softly, standing up from sitting, looking down at her. "Always remember Mary, we all face events in life that we don't want, but it's all a part of God's plan for something greater."

Mary just glared at him the whole time he spoke, not even acknowledging the things he said. "I would like you to leave."

Bishop David heard her request and nodded softly, walking away from where they were at and leaving the house.

She had watched him leave through the windows before she finally reached for her knitting needles and quilt, continuing to knit as she thought about what he said about God having a plan for everyone. To her, God's plan was killing William and taking away something that she loved most in the world, when she didn't have anyone else.

"Forget God." Mary said to herself quietly, having completely lost faith and love in God.

Chapter III

One stormy night soon had arrived in Lancaster County. Rain had arrived over the town and fields, the sound of sharp pellets hitting the roofs and windows of each building. The window whirled between each building, the sounds of wind wailing could be heard by anyone who was awake.

While the storm stayed present in the county, Mary was asleep in her bed, although she wasn't sleeping soundly. The red-headed woman was having a nightmare, causing her to toss back and forth in her sleep before some sort of sound interrupted her slumber.

KNOCK KNOCK KNOCK

Mary sat right up from her bed like a vampire in a coffin, rubbing her eyes. "What on Earth?" She said to herself, looking around the room as she wondered what caused her to wake up.

KNOCK KNOCK KNOCK

This time, the red-head heard the solution to the noise. "Who could be at my door in the middle of the night?" Mary got out of her bed, wrapping her blanket around herself to cover her nightgown. She made her way down the stairs of her home before seeing the front door. Once she got to the door, she slowly opened it, seeing who it was.

There was a man, about her age, with a young daughter about six-years-old. They were wet from head to toe, shivering as they looked at Mary.

"Please...do you have room in your home for my child and I? We come from far away to Lancaster County...we have no home, no food." The man said, his tone being a desperate one.

Mary had no idea that this was what waited for her on the other side of the door. "I...Well..." She looked at the two before she finally nodded quickly, stepping out of the way.

"Oh thank you...thank you!" The man said happily and emotionally. He quickly moved inside, Mary shutting the door behind the two. Even though they were inside, away from the rain, they still were shivering in the dark home. Mary saw how cold they were and immediately knew what they needed.

She quickly went over to the fireplace in the living room, taking two logs that were on the side of the hearth in a pile and putting them inside the fireplace. After a few attempts of trying to get a fire started, she eventually managed to do so, an orange glow illuminating the living room.

Once the man saw the fire, he moved his daughter close to the fireplace, trying to get her as warm as possible. Mary saw what he was trying to do and quickly went over to the eight-year-old, wrapping her blanket around the child. The man soon began to dry off her daughter while at the same time trying to get her warm.

"There you go...nice and warm now. Away from the cold rain." He said quietly to his daughter, holding her close as he sat in front of the fireplace with her.

The daughter shivered still, but the warmth from the fire and the blanket caused the shivering to decrease as the time went by.

Mary stood behind the two, watching them and making sure that they were okay. "Are you warm enough?" She asked them, having held one of the quilts she had made in her hands to give to the man.

"Yes...thank you kind miss." He said quietly, holding his daughter close before taking the quilt from Mary, wrapping it around himself.

With the two warming themselves up from the fire, Mary decided to grab another quilt for herself before sitting down on her couch. She wrapped the quilt around her body so she could be warm too. Since she now had two "guests" in her home, she didn't want to go upstairs, back to bed, with the knowledge that two strangers were downstairs in her home, two people who she had no idea who they were.

"Maybe they're thieves," Mary thought to herself, studying the two strangers. *"Although...she looks pretty young to be a thief."* She finally

decided to speak up, wanting to figure out who they were. "Where did you two come from?"

The man looked back at her, hearing her question before he began to reply to her. "We came from Somerset County." The man answered, still trying to warm up his daughter.

"Oh...that's far from here." Mary replied, sitting down on her couch, looking at the man.

"It very much is..." The man nodded, looking at her. "Do you know if there's any housing here in Lancaster County?"

Mary heard her question before she shrugged. "I'm not too sure. Are you looking for a place to stay?"

The man nodded, looking down at his daughter. She had fallen into slumber and had a warm expression on her face and had stopped shivering, indicating she was no longer freezing. "Yes."

She heard him and asked some more questions in order to get to know him. "Why Lancaster County? I'm sure there's plenty of other settlements along the way."

"I just," The man began to say, rubbing the back of his neck nervously, "I don't know...I guess I've heard a lot of great things about Lancaster. Figured that it would be a great place for my daughter to grow up in."

Mary nodded when he stated that it'd be a good place for his daughter to grow up in. "Lancaster really is a nice place to grow up in...a good place to start a fam-" she began to say before stopping when she was about to say "family." It reminded her of what she has always wanted to have and that made her think of William and her. "Well, it's a good place to meet nice and caring people."

The man saw her reaction when she was talking about family, but decided not to question it in order to remain polite. "That's good to hear...by the way," the man began to say, looking at her once again, "what is your name?"

She heard him and replied softly. "Mary...my name is Mary Lee Warner."

When the man heard her, he smiled softly. "That's a beautiful name."

Mary smiled softly when he complimented her name. "What about you? What's your name?"

"Robert." He said quietly, before looking down at his daughter, gently stroking her hair. "The little one is Miriam."

Chapter IV

The next morning had arrived, the rain was now gone, the only trace of rain being the puddles in the dirt. Mary decided to help Robert and Miriam out by going down to the church to see Bishop David could help them out.

Entering the church, there were only a few people present in the pews, praying to the Lord about whatever comes to their attention. Bishop David was not preaching, considering it was a Tuesday, so chances were he was at his home.

"Doesn't look like he's here." Mary said, turning around and leading Robert and Miriam out.

"Who are we looking for exactly?" Robert said, holding his daughter's hand as they walked towards Bishop David's house.

"We're looking for David, Lancaster County's bishop. He might be able to help you out with moving here." Mary replied, reaching the bishop's house before knocking on the door. Not too long after the knock, the door opened, Bishop David standing there.

"Mary?" He said, a little surprised. "What brings you here today?"

Mary explained the whole story to him, telling the bishop that Robert and Miriam showed up in the middle of the night, needing a place to stay and that they wanted to move to Lancaster.

"I see..." Bishop David said quietly, scratching his beard as he thought about it. "Unfortunately, there isn't any houses available right now."

Mary heard the news and let out a quiet groan. "So where will they stay if they don't have a home?"

Bishop David heard her before looking at the two, looking at Mary again. "Can I talk to you privately Mary?"

Mary was confused as to why, but nodded as she stepped inside the bishop's house. "What did you want to talk to me about?"

Bishop David looked at her before he let out a quiet sigh. "I wanted to talk to you privately about where they're going to stay. I believe they should continue living at your house until a new house can be built here in the county."

She listened to what he said before hearing his statement about the two staying at her home. "What? No. I can't have people living at my house."

Bishop David gave her a confused look. "Why not? You have one of the biggest houses here in Lancaster County. You're not living with anyone. There's plenty of room in the house for someone."

"Because, I don't have enough food to feed two more people. I don't want to start housing people." Mary was quick to say, folding her arms. "I can't let strangers come into my home and make themselves acquainted to the hou-"

"Mary." Bishop David interrupted, clearly showing he was getting irritated with her. "Enough with the excuses. I'm not going to force you to let them in. I'm only suggesting you give the two of them a home. It's not permanent, but where else are they going to go?" He asked Mary, looking at her with a serious expression. "They can't move into anyone else's home. They all have families, rather large ones too."

She listened to him, looking into his eyes as she thought about everything he was saying. Bishop David was right in many ways. Most families in the county had large families, homes that were already crowded. With Mary's house, it was just her. He even said that it wasn't permanent, so it'd be something that Mary didn't have to deal with for too long.

"I guess...I could have them stay for a little while." Mary finally admitted, realizing that she could be a little generous.

"Thank you Mary." Bishop David said before leading her back outside, now facing Robert. "We will discuss adding a house whenever I meet my colleagues. Until we can get a house added to the county, you'll have to stay with Mary for the time being."

Robert listened to what Bishop David said, nodding softly. "Okay, thank you."

Bishop David smiled softly, heading back into the house before closing the door.

Robert and Miriam turned toward Mary, looking at her. "So...are we going to back to the nice lady's house?" Miriam asked her father.

Mary heard her and couldn't help but smile. "Yes...yes you are."

Robert watched the two interact before he couldn't help but smile, seeing this stranger being so nice to his daughter.

"Alright. Let's head back to the house so I can get a room prepped up for you two." Mary said, clapping her hands together when she knew what she needed to do.

Chapter V

A couple of months passed by in Mary's household. The two strangers that had showed up on her doorstep were now friends of hers, having brightened up the household little by little. As Mary got to know Robert, he started feeling more and more comfortable around him, the two even joking around with each other.

With Miriam, she started to look up towards Mary as a mother figure, every now and then the little girl called Mary mom. Mary would hear this and laugh, finding it humorous that Robert's daughter called her mom.

While everyone was getting along just fine, Mary started to remember William again, every time she looked at Robert. There was something about Robert that reminded her of William. It might've been the way he made her laugh or the way he showed kindness to people. Whatever it was, Mary could see William through Robert, which made her think about if she found another William in her life.

It was now 6 PM and Robert and Miriam had finished eating dinner with Mary. When they finished, Robert decided to take Miriam to bed, since she started dozing off during dinner. Once she was in bed, she was out cold.

"She must've been really tired today. Miriam never goes to bed this early." Robert said, walking back into the kitchen. "I don't blame her...she didn't sleep that well last night."

"Oh poor thing." Mary said, cleaning the dishes in the sink. "I hope she rests well tonight."

"She probably will." Robert said, walking over before leaning against the counter. "So...what do you want to do?"

Mary continued to wash the dishes before she stopped, soon looking at him. "What do you mean?"

"Well I mean...Miriam is in bed early. Do you want to go out for a walk?" Robert replied, looking at her and waiting to hear an answer.

She looked at him before looking down at the dishes, thinking about his offer before setting the plates down. "I would enjoy that."

He smiled brightly before he walked out of the kitchen, planning on getting his jacket.

———

It didn't take long before the two were on an adventure, walking around the county in the early evening. The sky was an vibrant orange, the sun easing itself behind the hills.

"Wow...that's a beautiful sunset." Robert said softly, looking at it.

"It sure is." Mary said quietly, looking at it before she looked at Robert. With the two of them having grown closer, she soon started to think more in regards of making their relationship a bit more than friends. "Can I show you something?"

Robert heard her, turning his head and looking at her before he smiled softly. "Yeah of course."

Mary smiled brightly before leading him into the woods, walking in a certain direction. As for Robert, he wasn't sure where she was taking him, which made him a little nervous. Eventually, the two arrived in a rather large open area in the woods, a grass area that was decorated with wildflowers.

"Wow..." Robert quietly said to himself, stepping forward and starting to walk towards the flowers. "They're beautiful."

Mary stood behind Robert, watching his response before walking with him again. "I know. I love coming to this place. It reminds me of so many happy memories." She said before she began to lay down in the grass, looking at the sky that had become as orange as a Doris Longwing Butterfly's wing.

Robert watched what she did before he followed her actions, lying next to her as the two watched the sky. "You have quite the spot...especially one that you value." He smiled softly, relaxing on the grass.

The two watched the sky for a few, enjoying the time to relax with each other. Eventually, Robert spoke up, a question that had been resonating within him.

"How come you didn't want to let us live with you a few months ago?" He quietly said, still looking at the sky, some clouds gently moving along in the sky.

Mary heard him and gave him a confused look. "What do you mean?"

"You were talking to Bishop David the morning after the rainstorm. You told him that you didn't want anyone staying at the house because you didn't have enough food and didn't want housing people. Part of me though doesn't believe that."

Mary listened to what Robert was saying, her expression staying confused before her expression became more of a look of hesitant.

"There's something more than not enough food and not wanting to house people huh? You don't have to tell me, but just know I'm here if you want to talk." Robert said quietly, wanting to assure that she could trust him.

She listened to what he said before she began biting her own lip, thinking to herself before she let out a quiet sigh. "There is...there's a lot more to it. I think it's fair that you should know."

He heard her response to his question and turned onto his side, looking at her now as she began to speak about what the reason for not wanting anyone to live with her.

"It all has to do with a man I loved...a man named William." Mary said quietly.

Chapter VI

William Bradshire...a carpenter of Lancaster County. Most of the county knew him as the kind man who cared about everyone around him, even the ones who didn't care for him. William was the prime example of what it means to follow Christ's footsteps. He showed a strong love towards God, helped out around his community, showed love towards everyone, taught the youth about the Bible, and that's just the peak of the iceberg.

Sometimes in life though, bad things can occur that change one's life. For William, it was losing his parents at the age of eighteen. With his parents gone, he now owned the house, but that meant nothing to William. For a long time, he had struggled with the fact that his parents were gone, but during this time, he still continued to help people, having put them first before himself.

A great example of William putting others first was one cold, dark night. There was a knock on his door, the knock having echoed the entire silent household. When William opened his front door, he found a shivering girl his age, looking up at him. This girl was Mary.

The young girl had ran away from home, angry at her parents and her peers around her community. She was looking for a place to stay, which was she ended up on William's doorstep, a stranger to him. William was caring enough to immediately let her in; he even allowed her to stay as long as she needed. Even though she could've left any time, she found herself a priceless friendship.

Eventually, as time progressed, the redhead soon fell in love with William, the same happening with the boy. The two ended up revealing their love for each other when they discovered and rested in the grass area in the woods with the wildflowers. Ever since then, they were two peas in a pod.

As time progressed, they became closer and closer, almost being one soul. Mary began helping out in the community with him while developing a strong love of God since William introduced her to Him. Eventually, William decided that he was going to ask Mary for her hand in marriage, but his colleagues asked for his help in finishing the construction of a barn.

Unfortunately, William never had the chance to pop the question due to the accident. While he was watching his colleagues raise one of the barn walls up by pulling it up with ropes, the ropes snapped and the wall soon fell on William, his chances of escaping the wall very low with how fast the whole situation took. Sadly, William didn't survive the heavy barn wall crushing him.

Word soon got out around the county about William dying from the accident, which Mary soon heard about. She was devastated, crushed, her heart torn into pieces for the loss of her one true love.

After William had passed, Mary was given the house, considering she basically lived there and was a member of the community. During this time, Mary closed herself off from the rest of the world, locking herself away in her home, mourning the loss of William. She even decided to not let anyone into the house after the loss in order to keep the house peaceful, like it was when William and her were in it.

Even in the present, Mary still has nightmares about the whole incident, nightmares that remind her of the loss of William.

"If only I were there to stop him...to get him out of the way...If only I were there...he'd still be alive."

Chapter VII

Once Mary finished telling Robert the story, she had developed some tears from the memory of William's death.

"Now you know why I don't let anyone into the house...I know...it sounds insane, for the girlfriend of someone who has departed to keep the house like a temple. You must think I'm crazy..." Mary said quietly, wiping her tears.

"Oh no..." Robert said, looking at her. "I don't think you're insane at all...I can see why you value the house so much. All the memories with William...the laughter...the peace...everything about it...you don't want anyone to ruin this place for you." He said softly, gently resting his hand on hers. "I'm sorry...I didn't know this was the reason why you didn't want us here."

Mary heard him and finally broke down, tears rolling down her cheeks as she covered her face with her hands, muffled crying heard behind it. Robert reached for her and wrapped his arms around her, holding her close as he embraced her.

"Shhh...it's okay...Mary." Robert quietly said, stroking her hair gently to calm her down. "It's okay..."

After years of suppressing the memories of William and her, the pain she has endured from remembering his death, the many tears she had held back, she finally broke down and let her tears flow.

"I miss him so much...every day I wish I could see him again...tell him that I wish I could've saved him from the wall...I wish I could've done something." She said, pressing her face against Robert's shoulder as she shook from her crying.

"You couldn't do anything Mary...you had no idea that would happen..." Robert said softly, continuing to hold her close as she cried against him. "Look on the bright side...with William having a strong love for God, he's finally in Heaven where he can be with God...walk along with him...talk to him...laugh with him."

With Robert's words entering Mary's ears, it made her cry more. He was right in the sense that she wouldn't have known and that he's in a better place now. Her heart ached as she recalled all the memories of William from when they met to his death. All the memories were mainly happy and ones that would make her laugh whenever she looked back to them. Even though William was gone, she remembered one thing...William lives on through her. The memories, the house, the ideology, everything that William was made up of lives on through Mary. With this thought, she felt like she could finally get over the tragedy of losing William and achieve peace.

"Thank you...Robert...Thank you." Mary said quietly, looking up at him with tears in her eyes.

Robert looked down at her, confused as to why she was telling him thank you. "For what?" He laughed gently, wiping the tears away from her eyes.

"For saying all of those things about William and I...I've spent all these years holding onto William's tragedy and blaming myself for not being able to help him, but now I can finally find peace and let go of the tragedy...thank you...Robert." She finally said, looking at him as she gently reached up, stroking his cheek before she finally decided to lean in, kissing him gently.

Robert was caught off guard with the kiss, his eyebrows raising as she held her in his arms. Eventually, she broke the kiss, resting her head on his should. "Let's go back home...it's getting late." Mary said quietly, her eyes now closed.

Even though Robert had thought about pushing their relationship to another level, there was something that was holding him from reaching that level, something that had followed him from his previous home.

Chapter VIII

Many weeks had passed by since Mary told Robert about her past. Mary was in a much brighter mood, slowly building herself up again by socializing with people, going to church again, which made Bishop David happy, and she started wearing colorful clothes again.

Robert was thinking about what Mary had done in the wildflower area in the woods on the porch. He wanted to moved towards the next step, but the past was catching up with him.

"Hey!" Mary called out, coming up to the house with Miriam. "We've got dinner!"

He snapped back into reality, smiling gently when he saw the two. "Oh...that's wonderful. Looks delicious." Robert said, standing up and helping them take the food inside the house.

"I decided to cook something special for you...to thank you for helping me return back to my old self again."

Robert smiled and chuckled nervously, rubbing the back of his neck. "Oh...you don't have to do that."

"But papa," Miriam spoke out, looking at him, "look at the food! It looks delicious! At least let mom...Mary cook it for me."

Both Robert and Mary laughed at Miriam's comment, Mary picking her up and holding her.

"Okay, well if Robert doesn't want his special dinner, then I'll cook it for you." She said, walking in with the child.

"That'd be fantastic!" Miriam exclaimed happily.

Robert followed behind the two with the groceries, his expression being lost in thought as he thought about the past.

Dinner time soon arrived, everyone now seated at the table as they waited for Mary to come in with the special dinner.

"Whatever she's cooking, it smells delicious." Miriam said, excited to eat.

In a matter of minutes, Mary came out with a cooked turkey, the skin being a golden crisp.

Even though Robert wasn't asking for a special dinner, he was impressed with how the turkey came out. "Wow, looks really good Mary."

She smiled brightly, setting the plate down. "Well I'm glad you like it so much. I've got more coming out. I cooked some corn, made so mashed potatoes, have some greens." Mary explained to them as she walked back into the kitchen.

It took a few trips for her before she finally could sit down at the table with the two. "Alright, dig in." Mary said, taking her knife and fork, cutting into the turkey and scooping up a little bit of everything.

The dinner that they had all together was nice. Lots of laughter, lots of compliments, complete joy filled the room between Miriam and Mary, although Robert was most of the time quiet. After dinner, Miriam decided to go play with her doll in the living room while Mary and Robert were in the kitchen, cleaning the dishes.

While they were in there, Robert remained quiet, lost in his thoughts as he kept trying to shake it off. It didn't take too long though for Mary to see something was bothering him.

"You've been awfully quiet this evening...is there something wrong?" Mary asked him, continuing to wash the dishes.

"No." Robert said vaguely, not wanting to get into what was bothering him.

"You sure?" She said softly, looking at him. "You seem like you're thinking really hard about something."

"Don't worry about it." Robert said to her, trying to avoid explaining his thoughts.

Eventually, Mary let out a quiet sigh before setting her dish down, turning toward Robert.

"You know if something is troubling you, you can te-" Mary began to say to him.

"Drop it." Robert said harshly, looking at her for a few quick seconds before he finally set his plate down, shaking his head. "Just forget it...I'm going to bed." He said, leaving the kitchen and walking upstairs.

Mary was shocked by the way Robert reacted, considering it wasn't normal for Robert to be this way.

Miriam heard the commotion from the living room, looking at Mary. "Is papa upset about something?" She said with a concerned voice.

Mary heard Miriam and shook her head. "Don't worry about it dear. He just needs some time to himself."

Chapter IX

Robert currently laid in Mary's bed upstairs, his eyes closed as he tried sleeping. He didn't mean to snap at Mary, but considering his thoughts were getting to him, it was bound to happen. As he attempted to sleep, he soon felt something lay next to him, which interrupted his slumber. He opened his eyes and turned to look and see if it was Mary.

Of course, he was right in this situation. Mary was in her nightgown, having crawled in bed with Robert, getting cozy. Once he saw it was Mary, he returned back to his previous position, his back facing her. Still trying to avoid breaking the news to Mary, he soon felt her arms around his stomach, her body soon pressing against his back.

"What's going on with you? You're usually not like this." She said softly, resting her head against his back.

"I don't know Mary...I don't know." Robert said quietly, his eyes still closed.

"I feel like you do know Robert." Mary finally said. "I just feel like you don't want to tell me what you're thinking of."

He heard what she said, but didn't reply to it. The only thing he did was sit in silence with his eyes closed, trying to fall into slumber.

"You know I'm here if you want to tell me what's bothering you. I think it'd be healthy if you did though because you won't get any sleep with you thinking about whatever you're thinking. I know from experience." Mary quietly said, now closing her eyes as she rested her head against his back.

Robert listened to what she was saying before he let out a quiet sigh, trying to think about how he would explain his thoughts to her. Eventually, he decided to be straightforward with her.

"You know why I decided to move to Lancaster County?" He asked Mary quietly.

She merely shook her head against his back, indicating that she didn't know why he moved here. "Aside from finding a new home, no I don't."

Robert listened to what she had to say before he continued. "I left my previous home because my wife walked out on Miriam and I."

When Mary heard this, her eyes opened up and she sat up, looking down at him. "What? That's horrible! Why would she do that?"

Once Mary sat up, Robert turned so that he was laying on his back, now looking up at her. "To be honest...maybe I married the wrong person. She just...everything seemed fine to me. She was a good mother, I was a good father, we lived a happy life, but then one day..." He said before stopping, thinking back to that day before telling Mary what happened.

"Sara?" He called out, looking around his home. "Where are you?

While he walked around the house, Miriam watched him, not understanding what was going on. "Papa? What's going on?"

"I can't find mom. She's gone." Robert said, his tone being a little more scared. "Maybe she left something saying where she went. Yeah...she leaves notes."

"Maybe...I'll help you try and find something" Miriam said, getting off of the couch before walking around their home, trying find anything that could lead to the mystery of where Robert's wife went.

Eventually, Miriam found a note that had fallen on the side of the bed. "Papa!" She called out. "I found a note!"

Robert immediately ran into the room, seeing the note in Miriam's hand. He took the note from her and began reading it. Although the hope he had on his expression when he found the note soon faded the more he continued to read it. In fact, he soon had become emotionless from what was written on the note.

"What does it say papa?" Miriam asked, looking up at him.

Robert finished reading the note, looking down at Miriam before folding the note in half, tucking it into his pocket. "Don't worry about it sweetheart. I think though...we need to move away from this county."

When Miriam heard this, she was completely confused. "Why? Why do we need to move?"

He heard her before he picked her up, looking around the house one last time. "Because I think we will find somewhere else that'll be better for the both of us."

"We basically left the county with nothing but the clothes on our back. I couldn't stand living in the same county as her and live in a house that we lived in together." Robert said quietly, looking at Mary as he finished explaining his story. "Would you stay in the same place if you found out your love left you and your child for someone else?"

When Mary heard this, she let out a depressed sigh. "No...I don't think I would." She said quietly. "Is that what's been on your mind today?"

Robert heard her before nodding softly. "I've been thinking about it for a long time now...I've wanted to move onto the next step in our relationship, but...I fear that something would happen again...I fear the odds of you walking out on us."

Once Robert said that, Mary spoke up in a more serious tone. "Robert...look at me."

Robert did as told and look into her eyes, seeing what she would say.

"I would never do that...ever in my life." Mary said, looking at him as she gently rested her hand on his cheek. "I wouldn't do something to hurt you and Miriam...I love you both, with all my heart." She said to him before she gently kissed him, breaking it soon after before resting her head on his chest. "You don't need to worry about me every walking out on you two...I care about you two so much that my heart aches. I wouldn't even think about walking out on you two."

When Robert heard this, he let out a relieved sigh, his arms wrapping around her and hugging her against him. "I love you so much Mary..."

"I love you too Robert..."

THE END

ROLLING HILLS

SHELLY MCDONALD

I drove by an old torn up sign that read "Sugar Grove, Pennsylvania: Population 566." I turned down two side streets and made a left on Trout Avenue before I found a beautiful yellow cottage that sat on Danbury Lane; outside I saw the lawns were freshly manicured and flower pots with garden gnomes took up the empty space. There were vines growing up the cottage and there was a small swing that sat by an old oak tree. I looked up at the sky and saw the sun beginning to set over the hills. I looked over at the neighboring farms and saw cows grazing in the fields nearby. I closed my eyes and listened to the animals chattering about. Other than that, silence filled the air.

I didn't come to this small town to find a cowboy, I came here because I lack emotion. I feel that has to do with a certain woman. Although, one could think the emotions forming inside me was the start of a new relationship. I was both anxious and excited except those feelings were about finding my birth mother. I slaved many late night hours working as a waitress at a small diner making trash for tips. I was grateful for the hard work because it prepared me for college. I aced my way through grad school and ended up landing a job at the LA Times. I was pretty much the paper boy but it was something. It was all that work that got me to where I am today. I skipped any romantic entanglements because I was determined to hunt this woman down and that is hard enough because she comes from a community that doesn't use technology. Lately, I had been feeling lonely. Most of my friends had gotten married and had children by now. I was a lost cause, I guess. I chose the thrill of a career over romance and diapers. I put off my search until recently because it made me feel weak. My only thoughts were about school and work. In order to be great, I needed to shut off my feelings. That was until I landed this job and my boss told me I'm like an onion and not in a good way. The layers are apparently thick and under ripe. He told me to take a vacation and find true emotion.

I walked through the door expecting the cottage to be full of floral arrangements, but I was welcomed by a small kitchen that was connected to the living room. The walls were painted a sky blue and trimmed in white. The pictures on the wall were of sunflowers and honeybees. I saw a small white couch and a small blue chair that faced a television set. A small table, sat between the two chairs, contained a sunflower shaped lamp. A blanket hung over the chair appeared well worn from many years of use. A small dining room table separated the two rooms. At the back of the cottage was a large bedroom. The room held a king size feather bed with all white linen, a large chest of drawers holding a large mirror. In front of the mirror were empty storage containers that were to be filled with my belongings. I glanced at the paintings that hung on the wall. Most of the paintings throughout the house were of beautiful sceneries.

My stomach started grumbling so I headed back towards the kitchen. I was scrounging through the cabinets when I noticed it had been stocked with groceries. A note hung on the fridge from the owners that my assistant had called and arranged for them. I reached for an apple and checked my email. I sent a short message to my boss before I called Rhonda and thanked her for the kind gestures.

It was almost 7 pm and that apple didn't curb my hunger so I decided to look through the contents of the kitchen. Pasta always sounded good and with all the Italian ingredients I saw I decided to whip something easy up. I pulled out some fresh basil, a few Roma tomatoes, a bunch of linguini pasta, and a splash of olive oil. She ended up making Tomato Basil Pasta. I grabbed the remote and sat down at the table and searched the movies on television. I found nothing and opted for classical music and enjoyed the melodies. It cleared my head of all that useless inner babble that seemed to cloud my mind. I was looking out the window and I saw 3 younger kids riding their bikes as an older walked behind them. The older one was reading a book as she walked. She kept stumbling because her mind was obviously in a far off land.

The next day I headed into town to stake out the local bakery. I parked across the street from the bakery. When I stepped in front of the building and took the site in I saw a historical sign that read, "Amish Bakery founded in 1848 by Tobias Hochstetler. The structure was crafted out of natural wood and the window panes had flower boxes carved into them. The word "Bakery" was crafted out of white wooden blocks and plastered on the side of the building. There were fresh flowers in the boxes and the lawn was beautifully tailored. I liked the wooden picnic tables that sat on the front lawn for those who wanted to enjoy the fresh outdoors.

However, I smelled treats baking indoors and that was where I wanted to be. I smelled various bread baking in the large cast iron ovens. Another whiff told me that stew was simmering in pots on the stove in the back. I found a small table in the back. I looked around for a plug remembering Amish had no power which meant no plugs.

I was grateful for my two battery banks or writing was going to be a drag. I was looking around when I noticed the tables each contained a simple vase with a small bouquet of fresh wildflowers sat in the center of each simple table cloth; silverware was already placed out on each table, they were neatly tucked into their napkins. The tables looked hand carved and the decoration that hung appeared homemade. A large quilt was mounted on the wall and it took my breath away. Each stitch was hand stitched by the women of this community. Each block contained a little something from its artist. The squares were beautifully stitched together into one large quilt and presented to the Hochstetler's.

I took notice that people were walking through the doors and taking seats at various tables. The female patrons were dressed in calf length dresses that were of a solid color. Some of the dresses were eggplant in color, but most blues and greens. The women I noticed wore black bonnets over a white prayer cap. They paired their outfit with a pair of black boots. I noticed the men wore light colored shirts and dark pants. They had suspenders that held their pants up. I didn't see a single speck of metal on a single person. When the men entered the bakery they removed their hats and placed them on a rack at the front of the establishment.

It was only a matter of time before the place was almost full. I couldn't figure it out but there was something strange. I finally figured it out the strange thing was called silence. I was in an extremely busy establishment and there wasn't commotion coming from the kitchen or in the dining area. Everyone appeared to be either being working as a team or speaking in hushed tones. The employee's smiles appeared genuine as they greeted each table. I was amazed at how different service was compared to back in the city where people were shouting and their children were climbing over the tables. People always complain about their food in a city.

The waiter came up to my table and greeted me as he did the others. He too was dressed in plain fashion. I looked past his clothes and right into his sea green eyes. I noticed his hair was cut into a shaggy style and his front tooth was slightly out of line. His skin held a golden hue from long hours of working in the sun. He cleared his throat reminding me that he was standing in front of me.

"Hello My name is Abram and I'll be taking your order this morning, are you ready to order?" He repeated his question.

I nervously mumbled something about a breakfast puff, a banana, and a cup of coffee; managing to keep my head averted so that he wouldn't see the color forming its way onto my cheeks. He nodded as he stepped away.

I groaned in embarrassment as I took my simple black laptop from its well-worn bag. I started writing an article on school bus safety while I waited for my order. My boss must really hate me if I'm writing articles on bus safety. Apparently, bus drivers forgot there was such a thing because there has been a rise in bus accidents. I looked over my laptop and noticed some of the other patrons spoke quietly amongst one another, but when the food came they said a word of prayer and ate in total silence.

Abram brought my meal and asked, "Is there anything else I can do for you?"

I thought of many things he could do for me but instead replied with a curt "no thank you".

I glanced back and watched him walk away. I found that the service staff never left the front of the business. They stood at a podium and waited for tables that needed to be serviced. If a patron looked up the waiter was immediately there. No food was sent back and as the patrons left they all thanked the chef in German. I learned "denki" meant thank you and was pronounced "den-gee." Every single table wished to speak with the baker. At first, it struck me as an odd gesture but soon I realized the admiration these people had for this family.

I continued returning to the bakery every day for the next few weeks. I became fast friends with Hannah the female waitress and learned that 6-year-old Mary helped prepare meals when she was not in school. I speak with Abram when he comes by my table. He often gave me his million dollar smile and a quick wave before he went into the kitchen. Sometimes he stopped and chatted with me for a moment, so today when he did she wasn't nervous or scared.

"Hello Annabelle, Have you written any new articles lately?"

"I've written a couple here and there but nothing concrete. Thank you for asking."

"I was wondering if you had any plans tomorrow. I'd like to take you on a picnic."

I noticed his cheeks turn red. Wow.

I sat there frozen in my chair for a moment. I cleared my throat before speaking.

"I'd love too," I responded shyly.

Wildflower

The next day I was busy throwing clothes around the large bedroom so it didn't strike me as odd when I glanced around; a bra hanging from the ceiling fan and a sock fell from the lamp onto the wooden floor. I sighed and decided on a new outfit instead. I drove to a local boutique and bought a pair of capris, solid lavender top, and a white cardigan sweater. "This outfit will look super cute with the white low top sneakers I brought with me," I thought to myself. I pulled my cell phone from my bag and located the GPS app. I looked for a place to eat. I finally found something couldn't find my way back. I drove around for a while and eventually lost cell reception. I accidentally turned left instead of right and went up a hill where I hoped it would loop around but, it didn't instead the road just kept winding around. I wasn't able to turn around or I would have, so I continued driving until finally, I discovered a road that led to the main road. I screamed and yelled at the stupid reception in this little town but I drove another 10 miles before my GPS finally said turn right here and your destination is on the left. I growled at my phone before parking in front of the cottage. I was way behind on schedule. Abram was due soon and may have even left his home already.

I was finishing up my final touches when I heard trotting coming from down the road. I didn't want to seem eager so I left the screen door closed and sat on the couch to read a book. I opened the blinds up so I could see as he got closer. I felt the butterflies begin to swarm in my stomach as I watched the set of American Standardbred horses climb the final hill. I saw a green wagon trailing behind two horses. It was an open two-seater wagon, and even I knew that was more for romantic social calls. The butterflies turned up a notch. I stood and fixed a few strands of hair and checked my breath. I hadn't been on many dates in my life but I had a feeling this one was going to be life altering.

Abram helped me into his wagon and asked if I felt comfortable? Of course, I wasn't, but I'd never let him know that. The seat was hard and moved when I moved. The swaying of the moving wagon caused me to grip the side. Eventually, I got used to the motion and my heart stilled. The brisk northern breeze cooled my flushed face. The fresh air was inviting and it smelled sweet and of freshly cut grass. I had noticed the handcrafted bales of straw, and I was curious about how long it takes for them to do the whole field. I was seated next to someone who would actually answer me with an honest answer.

"Hey Abram, how long do it take to make the bales of straw?"

He spoke with a smile in his voice. "It takes one man many hours hacking the tall grass with a scythe but other farmers often pitch in and help one another. Some help even when they're unable to because they are gracious and kind individuals."

Abram called those individuals God's disciples. I stared at this man in awe. He was such a kind-hearted man. I loved hearing him praise his community like he did because whether he knew it or not he was one of those disciples. His story reminded me of the weeks I sat at the bakery and watched the Hochstetler's as they prepared each dish with joy and hard work. I realized then that the Hochstetler's were also disciples of God. I took a deep breath in enjoying the smell of freshly cut straw mixed with Abram's scent. He seemed to notice my hearty attempt at enjoying the scent of the countryside but didn't notice her feeble attempt at scooting closer. Abram drew in a deep breath and agreed the air was nice. Perhaps he too smelled the countryside mixed with the scent of her instead.

"Have you worked at the dairy farm you were telling me about?" I asked curiously.

"No I haven't, I will start back again tomorrow so I won't see you again until the weekend. I only work in the bakery when work isn't available elsewhere." He stated

A few moments later we pulled into a meadow filled with Eastern Daisies, Bearded Beggar sticks, swamp lilies, Bulbous Buttercups and Black-Eye Susan's. It was full of colors. I saw reds and greens with bursts of yellow and blues. In the center of the white Elderberry and Meadow Rue sat a colorful quilt with a hand woven picnic basket on top. I looked around and saw grasshoppers jumping around and blue and yellow butterflies danced through the sky. Blue birds sat on branches twittering about. I still couldn't believe it was quiet enough to capture moments like this one.

"Oh Abram, it's beautiful!" I cried

"I'm glad you like it. I wanted to find a place where I could get to know you." He confessed.

I laced our hands together and we walked towards the quilt. I brushed my hands along the flowers. I stopped to smell a few; I fell down when a lady bug tickled my nose. I stayed there in that spot and looked up at the sky. What was I doing? I was busy falling in love and I forgot about my mission to find Ruth Hershberger. For now, I was going to enjoy this but I needed to use the weekdays to find out how to get in touch with Ruth.

I stood up and I continued to look around. I took everything in because I wanted to remember this day for the rest of my life. I saw his green buggy on the hillside, the cedar, and the pine trees swaying in the distance. I saw butterflies and dragonflies dancing through the sky. I watched the grasshoppers jump from flower the flower. A laugh escaped my mouth as I twirled around like a child. I felt like I had the world at the tip of my fingers and it's all because of Abram. He talked with me and he listened to me. He paid full attention when I spoke. He never strayed from our conversations, and he never looked bored. He filled me with happiness and he made me feel special.

I walked over to the quilt and sat beside Abram. Together we talked about our hopes and dreams. I picked up a carrot and took a bite before asking him

"Are you happy where you are in life because I feel really lost?"

"I was lost for some time but I prayed that one day I would figure out what I wanted and I found it. I want to open my own furniture store. Why do you feel lost "liebchen"? He asked.

My eyes got teary and I finally told him the truth.

"I came to Sugar Grove in search of a woman. I'm using you the history of your family's bakery as my cover up. I'm trying to locate an Amish woman named Ruth Hershberger. I have some urgent information I need to discuss with her. She may be the woman who gave birth to me."

Abram pulled me into his arms and kissed my head. I melted into his warm embrace, he held me like that until I felt him shifting his body.

Abram laid his body down beside me and looked me in the eyes before he spoke.

"I promise that I'll help you in any way that I can."

"I know you will," Annabelle said truly believing his words.

Abram and I watched the sunset together. Our fingers danced together on the quilt. There were moments of silence but they were filled with laughter. Abram always knew when my mind began wandering. He always attempted to pull me back and I was thankful for the distraction. I saw the stars form in the sky and knew my night was drawing to an end.

"Do you write books? Abram asked me curiously.

"I haven't thought writing books lately but it was a dream of mine growing up," I confessed.

"Do you make things for entertainment or just tools and furniture?" I asked

"You called me something earlier, what was it again?" I asked

"I called you liebchen" he blushed.

What does liebchen mean? I inquired

"It means my love" he spoke confidently.

"Liebchen sounds better than my love if you ask me," I admitted.

I learned he wanted to work with animals and wished one day to be a veterinarian, but he understood that he couldn't afford school. He looked at the sky and announced it was time to start heading home. The buggy ride home was silent but in a good way. The ride home Annabelle could see fireflies lighting up the sky and she could hear crickets chirping in the night. This night felt too good to be true. It felt absolutely bewitching. When they made it to her cottage they heard an owl hooting nearby. Annabelle giggled and confessed she wasn't used to such beautiful noises. She was used to horns honking, sirens blaring, and the usual city noises. She started to enjoy looking up and seeing the constellations in the sky and hearing the animals and insects talk in the night. It felt like a whole other universe out here. Abram pulled up to the little yellow cottage on Danbury Lane and walked me to the door. He looked a little nervous before he finally spoke up.

"Would you like to attend Sunday Worship with my family? It is always nice to listen to the bishop tell tales about "Herr Gott.""

"Yes, I would love to join your family on Sunday." I eagerly responded.

"Perhaps you will see Ruth there." He spoke confidently.

"Perhaps I will."

Kiss Me

The week was long and brutal. I continued going to the bakery even though I knew Abram wouldn't be there. I managed to write send an article in and prayed it would hold over until I discovered the actual story I was searching for. I was glad Abram wasn't here because could focus on finding Ruth. I looked through the local phone book and found a Hershberger family lived in Sugar Grove. Their address was close by but I could feel myself cowering down. I also didn't want to march up to Ruth and say "hi might it possible that you carried a child 22 years?" I learned enough to know that the Amish were close knit and they weren't keen on outsiders meddling in their business.

I woke up early Sunday morning and took a bubble bath. I was daydreaming about spending the day with the Hochstetler's and learning about the Amish community that I didn't hear knocking on the door. I was in the middle of daydreaming when I heard a noise again. This time I drained the water and climbed out of the tub. I was putting my robe on when I heard my name being called.

"Annabelle, are you in there?" said a deep male voice.

I recognized that voice but I wasn't dressed to meet him at the door. I stood behind the closed door and answered back.

"Abram is that you?" I asked a little nervous

The last time I looked at the clock it had been 6 am. Who would be here so early?

"Yes, it is Abram are you alright?" He sounded scared.

"I just got out of the shower, I'm going to unlock the doors and go back to my room. Count to 60 and then you can come in." I said awkwardly

Abram busted out laughing and then I heard his faint counting. I ran to the back of the cottage and slammed the door closed. I grabbed my dress off of the hanger and threw it over top of me. I started pulling curlers from my hair when I heard water running in the kitchen. I was curious about that but opted to put on my shoes and fix my hair instead.

Abram helped me into the buggy. We trotted the three miles to his family farm and picked up his sisters Hannah and Mary. The girls looked a little flustered but neither said a word at first. Hannah broke the silence.

"Grosseldre and Maemm rode with Daed to the Yoder bauereie. "

Mary apologized when she interrupted her sister but she saw Annabelle's uncomfortable shifting.

"Hannah our guest doesn't speak Pennsylvania Dutch perhaps you should use Englisch."

Hannah's faced reddened before she apologized.

"Our grandparents rode with our parents to the Yoder Farm so we don't need to pick them up this morning."

"Mary that was kind of you to include Annabelle into the conversation, Herr Gott is smiling down on you for your acts of kindness." The young child's wise older brother acknowledged.

The buggy pulled onto a large farm and parked next to the other rows of wagons. The farm was beautifully maintained. She had noticed the clothes line pulley first, they were empty today. There are usually animals roaming about but today they were confined to the barn. Worship was held on that warm summer morning because there were 200 people that showed up to hear the bishop speak. After he finished speaking children began playing a game in a nearby field. Men helped with farm work as the women prepared the covered dishes. I saw the elderly in chairs and gossiping about the latest news.

The food tasted amazing but I enjoyed wandering around and meeting new people. I was so curious about their lifestyle so I excused myself to take a deeper look. I walked into the big red barn and walked past rows of cows, sheep, and horses. Occasionally I'd pick up some straw and feed an animal. She walked by a pen of baby pigs and melted. They were oinking and oinking. I left the barn and walked towards a tree covered area that separated the farm from the fields. I stumbled upon deer drinking from in a stream and fish skipping in the water. I saw spider webs with dew on them spread across some blackberry bushes. I pulled out my phone and captured the rare moments of beauty.

I was walking back to the others when I saw a woman who looked vaguely familiar. She was helping a small child fix their clothes near the outhouse. I waited until the child ran off before trying to speak with the woman. Maybe she knows Ruth or perhaps she is Ruth. There was something that was pulling me in the direction of that woman. I was about to greet her but she took one look at me and turned and walked away.

The pain felt was unimaginative. My guts hurt and I felt couldn't breathe, I looked for the only one who knew my secret.

"Abram, I am so sorry, but do you think you could take me home? I'm not feeling well." I asked teary eyed.

"I need to let my parents know but I'll meet you at the buggy." He said while walking towards his father.

Abram told his parents that he had to take me home because I was feeling ill. I looked at the row of buggies and was extremely lost. I found Abrams two horses and climbed into the buggy behind them. She was prepared to wait because she knew he was speaking with his family. I leaned forward and saw a tall gorgeous figured getting closer, so I stuck my head out and waved. He bellowed a deep laugh.

"Annabelle that's the wrong buggy Annabelle laughed so hard, but she swore those were his horses. She even fed them saved carrots from her meal.

When we got to my cottage Abram could feel I needed to talk so he asked if I'd like to take a walk. We were walking on the dirt road for a little while before he pulled me onto a walking trail. As we walked the trail Abram took my hand before speaking.

"What happened today at the Yoder farm?"

"I tried to speak to this woman who looked familiar, but she ran away."

I know it sounds childish but I believe it was Ruth.

We walked and talked for a while before Abram spotted a stream. He found a large leaf and made a bowl out of it so that we could enjoy the water. We were walking again this time he took her with confidence and kissed it. We walked for a long time before I asked,

"Are we walking to my home in LA?"

"Come we will rest before we head back to your house," Abraham laughed.

He was used to long hours of walking but he understood that she wasn't accustomed to it.

We walked into a hay field where they sat and rested while they talked. I pulled a piece of straw lose and gathered the courage to see where this relationship was going.

"Have you ever been in love?" I asked timidly

Abram smiled like he was just pondering the topic himself.

"Yes, I have been in love. This woman brightens the sky when she steps into the sunlight. She lights up a room when she walks in with a smile on her face. I hear her heart beats and my world feels absolute. She walks barefoot in the sand and has skin the color of caramel. Her eyes are the color of storm clouds on a hot summer's day. Her lips look like ripe cherries ready for tasting. Abram picked up his queen and placed her on his lap. He kissed me with more passion than I thought possible. He pulled me closer and continued dancing his tongue around in my mouth. I moaned and sank into his embrace. He held me tightly and deepened the kiss. Eventually, he pulled away and kissed my nose before he spoke again.

"Annabelle Michaels, I love you more than I ever thought possible. I'd rather die a lonely man before I'd ever give you up."

We had better start back before it gets too late. I have to work in the morning and you need to find Ruth.

Deception

The next morning I woke up feeling fresh and determined. I decided to take matters into my own hands. I am going to the Hershberger farm and meet this family. I pulled out a cookbook from the cabinet. I decided to make a chicken casserole to show respect for their family. It took me a few hours to get things together and it was almost lunch time. I loaded the rental car and drove to the address I found the other day.

I pulled up to the farm and knocked on the door. The paint was peeling from the wood and the hinges were rusted. There was a large run-down barn behind the house and there was a fenced off area on one side of the house. I knocked again and shouted a greeting. An elderly woman came to the door; she spoke little English and told me to go around back.

Annabelle walked over to the fenced area and shouted

"Hello is anyone here?"

I heard the woman talking to a man in hushed tones but the man turned and walked away, but not before I could see tension rise in his shoulders.

I took a deep breath and she walked up to the woman I saw the other day.

"Good Afternoon, I am Annabelle Michaels and I work with the LA times. I'd like to write a story on your dairy farm if that is ok with you. We want to determine if there is a large difference in the way milk is produced."

The woman chuckled before responding

"I know you came here because you want to know if you're my boppli. I know you want to know if I am your Maemm."

The woman interrupted Annabelle before she could speak. She took my arm and led me to where she was working. Together we talked and pulled weeds from her garden. She naturally chastised me when I was rushed.

"Ruth, didn't you want me for a child?" I dejectedly asked

All these questions started to form in my mind but right when I was about to ask with full confidence I looked up and I saw that golden hair that caught my eye my first day in this town.

I couldn't believe it Abram knew Ruth all along. I had to know why he didn't tell me but right now I just wanted him to know that I now know his secret.

I walked over to him and asked to speak with him alone. He said he needed to finish his shift and he would come to the cottage so we could talk.

I drove the 3 miles back to the cottage in tears, I had learned who Ruth was, and I learned Abram was manipulative and he kept things from those he loved. Neither obviously loved me or cared for me or they would have been honest from the start.

I curled up on the couch waiting to hear from the airlines. I was booking a ticket and getting out of this small town. I was watching reruns on TV when there was a faint knock on the door. I opened the door and there standing was not Abram but Ruth; her birth mother was standing right in her doorway. It was the one thing I always wanted and often dreamed of. I didn't care if I had the perfect man or the comfiest shoes. I just wanted to be accepted by the woman who gave up on me.

I invited Ruth in and listened to her tale that began 23 years ago. I learned my dad was a fisherman and my parents met when my dad delivered fish to the local market. He would often purchase jam from her mom's fruit stand and one time he bought all her jam. He stopped by each summer for three years before her mom finally grew the courage to leave her roots and locate the man that filled her soul. My mother found my father and she claimed he was the love of her life but she only had a few short months with him. She felt punished by god when they discovered he had colon cancer. Her mom had just discovered she was pregnant with Annabelle when her father told her the news. My father stayed with my mom for the first 2 months but when he died my mother was forced to live in a women's shelter until she gave birth. She put me up for adoption and when I was adopted Ruth moved back to her parents and joined the Amish church.

Ruth admitted that she never mentioned Annabelle until Abram confronted her a few weeks ago. Ruth learned Annabelle was getting impatient and wanted to meet her but Ruth was ashamed that she hid her secret for so long. That was when Ruth told her story to the community and to her husband. He knew of her relationship with Annabelle's father but he was unaware she conceived a child. Annabelle drew in a deep breath and immediately thought of Abram and how hard it must have been to confront Annabelle.

"Annabelle, Darling, do you know what your plans are? Are you playing games with Abram or are you prepared to join the church? Abram isn't going to leave his heritage, he knows what he wants. It's up to you to decide if this is the life for you."

There was a knock on the door and they both knew who it was. My thinking time was up but I was fairly sure I had my answer. I opened the door and ushered him to the swing that faced the hills.

"Abram, how long have you known about her being my mom?"

His shoulders sank then he fell to his knees. I saw tears escape his eyes, but there was no way I was going to let him get away that easily. No matter how much I loved this man, he kept something from important from the person he swore he loved.

"Liebchen, I realized the day that you mentioned your birth mother's name. I won't lie, I knew who she was, but I wanted to make sure it was the right person. I didn't want to accuse someone of something she never did. Once I discovered she was the woman you were searching for I asked her to come to you when she was ready because it's her news to share. I wasn't around then and I don't know much now. I do know that there is much she eager to tell and in time I'm sure she will. We both care deeply about you and are worried you will leave. I'm sorry I kept any information from you, I only did it out of protection."

I looked into his eyes as he faced me and I saw the same as when he told me about God's disciples. He was helping a friend in need, this friend just happened to be my mother.

I hadn't seen real emotion until I saw this man's face. It was full of emotions, guilt mixed with grief and a face stained with tears. He held onto my leg like it was the only thing holding us together. I could turn cold and run away but instead, I dropped to my knees and placed my head on his chest. All I wanted was Abram and Ruth in my life. I looked up and I kissed him hard. I fell into his arms and confessed.

"Abram Thomas Hochstetler "Ich liebe dich" than one could love one's self. I used the Dutch phrase for I love you trying to prove my devotion to his heritage. I think of you daily and I pray for your safety each night. I hold you in my heart where I've held no other. There is no way I would turn and walk away; I want to be a part of your life."

He looked at me and laughed a deep humble laugh and before I could interrupt him he took my hands in his and spoke softly.

"Annabelle Naomi Michaels Hershberger, will you marry me?"

THE WEDDING DRESS

GIGI GROSS

Chapter 1

Gabriela stared at her bank account, willing it to change. There was no way she was down to a hundred and twenty dollars. She wasn't getting paid for another three days! Even when she did get paid, a majority of it would get eaten up by her rent and groceries for that week. "Oh no," Gabriela said, laying her head on her arms. She didn't want to think about it, or look at it, or have anything to do with it. Unfortunately, when the problems are in your own life, you cannot exactly run away from them.

Gabriela wanted to call Bryan and get his support. She knew he would have all the verbal support she could want, but he wouldn't be able to loan her any money. His financial situation was just as bad as hers and he made even less money than she did. Once again, Gabby re-evaluated the idea of moving in with Bryan already. It would save them a few hundred bucks a month, and it wasn't so bad. After all, everyone was doing it.

"Maybe then, I would actually have money for a wedding dress," Gabby muttered to herself.

"Having a conversation with yourself again?" Reese asked her.

Gabby quickly minimized her bank account window. "Yes," she replied, trying to put aside her doubts to talk to her sister.

"You're starting to worry me. Turn that frown upside down!" Reese said, coming over and hugging Gabby.

Gabby couldn't help shaking her head and allowing a small smile to form on her lips. "Thanks, Reese." Reese started playing with Gabby's hair, brushing her fingers through its strands. Gabby closed her eyes and sunk into the sensation. It felt so calming to have her sister play with her hair as she had done since she was a little girl.

"Your graduation is in two weeks, isn't it?" Gabby asked, making slow conversation. Reese's hands felt so good.

"Yup! I can't believe I'm actually going to be done with high school. Then, I'm going to college, and that scholarship is seriously a blessing, don't you think?"

Gabby did her best at a nod. "Yes, I don't know how we would do it without that scholarship."

"Do you think Mom and Dad will come to my graduation?" Reese asked in a quiet voice. Gabby was glad she didn't have to look her sister full in the face as she answered.

"I don't know, Reese. Dad might not come because he thinks Mom will be there. Besides, he hasn't really been here for a while. I don't know. Mom might come."

"Do you think she'll bring her terrible boyfriend?"

"I don't know, Reese, but I want you to focus on your success, not on other people. You and only you have been the one responsible for getting yourself through high school. You have studied hard, and this is your time for a reward. I was thinking just you and me could go get ice cream at Scream Cream, maybe not that night but maybe the next if you are too busy partying."

Reese knew that Gabby's money situation was tight, but she just didn't know how tight. Gabby didn't dare let Reese in on the secret. They just needed to get through the summer then Reese would be in college, and Gabby would somehow pull together enough money for just a small wedding.

"When are you going to go dress shopping?" Reese asked after a few moments of silence.

"I don't know, Reese. I will be going soon. Don't worry. You will be invited."

"Yay! You know I am so excited for you! I'll still be able to come home for Thanksgiving or fall break to wherever you guys are, right?"

"Of course, Reese!" Gabby said, finally turning and looking her sister in the eye. "Come here." Even though Reese was eighteen, Gabby was still her big sister at twenty-five. "You will always be my baby," Gabby said, trying to make Reese sit on her lap.

"No!" Reese wailed. "I shall not! I am too old to be sitting on anyone's lap."

"Mmhmm," Gabby smiled mischievously. "I'll just tell that to your striking college boyfriend when you get him."

"Eww!" Reese said. "I'm not going to sit on anyone's lap."

Gabby laughed. "Sure, you say that now. Shall I videotape you saying it and show to you in five years? Come on, help me finish making that garlic bread."

Two days later, Gabby decided to pay a visit to Bryan. They wanted to have their wedding in the middle of August. At this point, they hadn't done anything more than decide it would be held on Bryan's family farm. That decision was based on the fact that it would be a free venue, including free flowers.

"Hey, Baby," Bryan said when Gabby dropped by at dinnertime. "I made something healthy for once. You should be proud of me."

Gabby laughed. "Of course, I'm proud of you. Reese and I rebelliously did not make a salad with our meal last night, so you are doing better than me."

"Come here," Bryan said, pulling her close. He gave her a sweet kiss. When he pulled back, Gabby smiled. This was why she was with him. He always made her feel at home. "Go ahead and sit down. I'll get you a drink in a minute," Bryan commanded.

Gabby took a seat and watched Bryan career around the kitchen, pouring drinks, draining whole wheat pasta, and preparing their plates. When they finally sat down, Gabby took his hand and listened to Bryan pray. "Thank you, God, for this meal you have given us the resources to have. Please keep giving us all that we need. Amen."

The two began eating, and Gabby finally got up the nerve to bring up the old wedding topic. "Do you think we will even be ready to get married in August? That's only two and a half months away. I'm just worried that we won't have everything ready."

Bryan sighed, but Gabby knew that his frustration was not aimed at her. "I know it's stressful. But, we've almost gotten the rings paid for." Gabby realized at that moment that she forgotten to bring her ring payment that evening.

"Sorry!" Gabby interrupted. "I forgot my payment tonight. I'm getting paid tomorrow, though. I can just give you the money then, right?"

Bryan nodded. "That's fine. I know you're tight too. But, look, we'll have a beautiful meadow, rings, our pastor will come, and gorgeous wildflowers. Maybe we can ask guests to bring a dish. I know it's not conventional," Bryan said in response to Gabby's strange look. "But, maybe they will understand. Feeding so many people can be a few thousand dollars."

"I know," Gabby nodded. "And you paint a beautiful picture. I like the way it sounds. The problem is that. . .I really want to wear a special dress. I've always dreamed of a gorgeous white wedding dress, and I just don't know if I will be able to afford one. I don't want our wedding to just pass by like it's not anything special. I want to look beautiful for you." Gabby's voice cracked with emotion, and she looked down to avoid crying.

Bryan reached over and pat her hand. "I know that it is important to you. It's important to me that you have the wedding just how you want it. But I want you to know that whatever you choose to wear, I will love it." That was when Gabby realized that her yearning to wear such a beautiful gown might not be because she wanted Bryan to think she was beautiful. Maybe she just wanted to feel beautiful for once, not for anyone else but for herself.

Chapter 2

On Saturday, Gabby left Reese sleeping at home in bed to peruse the local flea market. She needed to get Reese a graduation present, but she also didn't have a lot of money to spend on something like that. She had no idea what she wanted to get her sister, but she knew that she liked to read. Perhaps, Gabby could find a few books at a reasonable price.

Gabby was looking at a table of books, holding a couple in her hands. The three books were only twelve dollars altogether, and Gabby thought they would be a great present for Reese right before her last free summer. Gabby looked up, and her eyes fell on a shining white dress hanging on a mannequin the next stall over. Gabby left the three books on the table and walked toward the dress as if in a trance.

Her hand reached up to stroke the fabric. Just as her fingers were going to touch the fabric, Gabby wondered if she should. She looked around to see if anyone was watching her. She saw a small, elderly woman with her eyes trained on her.

"Oh, sorry," Gabby said, stumbling into an apology. "I'm sorry. I didn't know if it was alright to touch, but it's so.. .pretty."

"Go ahead," the woman said in a raspy but friendly voice. "You may touch it." Her smile encouraged Gabby just the bit she needed to have the courage. She turned back to the dress and stroked it. It was soft, almost like silk. The beadwork was amazing, with little detail stitched along the folds of the fabric. The bosom was covered with exquisite beadwork, and the waist came in before flowing out in a long skirt. The train was not overwhelming but still had a presence. It was as though someone had created a wedding gown out of Gabby's imagination.

Gabby's breath caught in her throat. She didn't want to turn away from the beauty. She stealthily scanned the dress for a price tag. Of course, there was not one. That must mean that the dress was handmade and would cost even more.

"Th-thank you," Gabby said, turning away from the dress and nodding to the woman. She took a backward step away from the dress and the woman.

"Are you getting married?" the woman asked, leaning forward encouragingly.

"Yes," Gabby nodded. "But, we don't have a date yet. It will still be a few months." Finally, she shrugged her shoulders and figured she might as well ask how much the dress cost. If she didn't, she would constantly wonder. At least with a number, she could walk away from it without feeling guilty. "How much is the dress?" Gabby nodded toward the wedding dress she had been studying.

The old woman smiled and leaned back. "Oh, that dress doesn't have a price. I'm sure you noticed. It is a beautiful and priceless piece. But," the woman continued speaking before Gabby could turn away. "I will let you wear the gown for free if you promise me one thing."

"What?" Gabby whispered, unable to wait to hear her words.

"You must live out your marriage according to God's will."

"I-uh-oh," Gabby seemed unwilling to respond. "I can wear it. . .for free?"

The woman nodded. "There's a veil that goes with the dress as well, but I must have you promise that your marriage will be uplifting to God. Can you do that?"

"I promise with my whole heart," Gabby said. She couldn't control the smile that spread across her face.

The woman nodded. "Very well. God, our good Lord, will hold you to your word. Now, just give me a moment to gather the dress and package it safely. Do you have a few minutes?"

"Yes, of course!" Gabby could hardly believe her good fortune. "Do you need any help? I could help you."

"That blue bag up there on the shelf, yes, that one. That's the veil. Go ahead and get that down, will you?" Gabby strained up to reach the high shelf, took down the bag, and could not help peering into the bag to examine the veil.

"What do you think?" the woman asked, nodding at the veil.

"It's amazing," Gabby said. The woman carefully took out the veil and used the comb part to place the veil on Gabby's head. She handed Gabby a small hand-mirror, and Gabby nearly cried. She looked like a real bride, not a bride who didn't have any money. Spontaneously, Gabby reached down and hugged the old woman. "Thank you," she sobbed out. The woman patted Gabby's back.

Finally, Gabby carefully folded the veil and put it back in the bag. She then helped the woman take the dress off the mannequin and store it in a garment bag.

"I have one more thing for you," the woman said as Gabby prepared to leave. The woman pulled out a thick book. "I want you to take a look at this. This dress, you see, has a long history. It has made many brides happy on their wedding day, and they all needed it in one way or another. I encourage you to find out about their stories and write your own as well."

Gabby took the thick, leather bound book in the crook of her arm and tried to give the woman one last hug while balancing her packages. "How will I find you again?" Gabby asked.

"I'm always right here," the woman assured her. "Come back after your wedding, and I'll be waiting."

Gabby smiled, thanked the woman one more time, then hurried out of the flea market, forgetting all about Reese's graduation present. The smile could not be wiped off her face. She carefully laid the dress across her backseat and could not help but sing along with every song on the radio. The only thing left to do was try it on. When she reached home, she carried the dress inside and explained the whole story to Reese who at first felt deceived that her sister had gone wedding dress shopping without her.

"I'm going to try it on," Gabby said. "Wait until I'm in it, okay? Don't come in!" Gabby shut the door with her sister outside and changed as carefully as she could into the wedding dress. Gabby could tell the dress had had sleeves at some point. But, it was now a sleeveless dress. The hem was a little long, but Gabby knew she could fix that. Around her waist, the dress fit perfectly. Gabby tucked the veil into place then opened the door with a smile.

"Sis!" Reese said. The smile filling her face was all that Gabby needed to see. "It's perfect isn't it?"

"Yes, it is!" Reese gave Gabby a hug. "I can't believe you are actually getting married!"

"It seems real now."

"It is real," Reese said. "I know Bryan would love you in this dress. I wish he could see it now."

"I know!" Gabby laughed. "But it has to be our secret. "No words to him about it. None, do you hear me?"

Later that night, Bryan came over. He got along well with Reese, and Gabby loved that about him. After all, she might not be Reese's official guardian, but she was Reese's home ever since their parents had started their incessant bickering.

The three were playing a game of Phase 10, and Reese kept smiling randomly at Gabby. "Is something wrong with you?" Bryan asked her. "Or do you two have a cheat going on?"

Both Gabby and Reese laughed. "Nope, we're not cheating," they said in unison.

"Okay, because that denial was totally believable. Come on, I know something is up." Gabby looked at Reese. They both shrugged, but Gabby could not longer keep the news in.

"I got my wedding dress today," Gabby said.

"What?! That's amazing, Gabby. Where is it? Can I see it? Was it expensive?"

"To all of those questions, the answer is no. Besides, the groom is never supposed to see the dress before the wedding day."

"I've got an idea," Bryan said, leaning forward. "Want to get married tomorrow?"

"Sorry," Gabby shook her head. "Pastor is occupied tomorrow. Besides, I'm not ready yet."

"Aw," Bryan visibly drooped. "I guess we should probably wait until we have rings, huh?"

"That would be important!" Gabby said. She gave Bryan a playful kiss and was glad that she did not feel as desperate for a dress as she had that morning.

Chapter 3

Gabby carefully opened the book the woman had given her the day before. In the excitement of trying on the dress and spending time with Bryan, she hadn't thought about it again until she and her sister were leaving church. She hadn't told her sister about the book or how exactly she had gotten the dress, but she had told her enough to be satisfied.

The book appeared to be some sort of journal. On the pages were handwritten notes, some in cursive, some printed, and clearly not all done by the same person. Beside each handwritten note was a picture of a woman wearing the wedding dress. Gabby ran her hands over the first picture. The dress had had sleeves, just as Gabby suspected. The picture looked old, and it was worn around the edges. But it had stayed faithfully in the book. Beside it was a note.

"Teresa Daniels, age twenty-four. Married to Bertram Frantz, age twenty-four, on May 7, 1978. My parents had both died when I was five. I had been living with a family friend since then. The boy I grew up living next to asked me to marry him, but I didn't have any money for a wedding, let alone a beautiful dress. I met this wonderful young woman who loaned me a dress that she had just finished making. She told me to tell my story and live my marriage in a way that would make God pleased with me. I am determined to do just that. My adoptive parents may not have enough money to pay for a wedding, but this wedding dress shows just how much God is looking out for us."

Underneath the note was Teresa Frantz's contact information. In different handwriting was a little note that said she had died in a car accident in 2004. Gabby suddenly felt as though she was holding something very sacred. The dress was only used perhaps once a year, if that, and Gabby hungrily read through each story. Each woman had something to say about how she did not have enough money or something had befallen her. Gabby wondered why their contact information was there. Did they really want someone to talk to them? And what did they want to talk about?

Gabby pictured herself eight years from now with a few small children. She would always remember how she had gotten her wedding dress. What would she say to someone else who was going to use it? Gabby could only smile.

She selected two of the most recent weddings and decided to write to their email addresses. Her message was simple.

"Hi, my name is Gabriela. I'm going to use the wedding dress. I found your information in the book, and I was wondering if you'd like to meet and have a coffee."

Gabriela went to bed at close to two in the morning. "I am so not going to be awake for work in the morning," Gabby said. She had received her payment in her account over the weekend, and Gabby spent a little time that Monday morning paying her bills. It was just as nasty as ever. Even though she had a wedding dress now, she still would not be able to save any money after paying everything necessary. She sighed and shook her head. "It's okay," she told herself.

The workday passed well enough, but Reese was celebrating when she got home because she only had two more exams before she was officially done with school. Gabby spent some of the evening quizzing Reese before she gave herself the luxury of checking her email. She had received a reply.

"It's nice to hear from you, Gabriela. I would love to meet for coffee. How does Wednesday at lunch hour sound? Would it be possible for me to meet you at the Starbucks in Clayton?

Annabel"

Gabriela rejoiced over the email. She couldn't wait to meet this woman and unravel a bit more of the dress mystery.

When it finally came time for her Wednesday lunch hour, Gabby drove as quickly as she could to the Starbucks. She ordered and looked around for Annabel. She finally found her, and the two shook hands in a formal manner.

"I'm so glad you reached out and contacted me," Annabel said. "I wondered if anyone ever would."

Gabby smiled excitedly. "I can't believe the dress was first loaned out in 1978. It still looks so new."

"Well," Annabel surmised. "The sleeves were taken off, and I think some extra beadwork was added."

"Still," Gabby smiled. "It's like I'm wearing a little bit of history."

Annabel laughed. "Yeah, it's magical the way that woman wants to help us. It's like she can just sense the desperation in someone."

"So, what's your story?" Gabby asked, wanting to fill in the blanks Annabel's note had left.

Annabel nodded. "I was eighteen when I got the wedding dress. I know, I was young. I didn't want to get married yet, but my boyfriend had gotten me pregnant. I had just found out a few days before. I had talked to my boyfriend, and he and I decided we would just have a quiet wedding, a justice of the peace deal. I didn't want to do that, but I knew we needed to do something quickly. I didn't want to be one of those boldly pregnant brides. But I was so frustrated with the whole situation, that I had just decided I would wear an old dress. It didn't matter.

"When I saw that wedding dress, though, I couldn't help but be drawn to it. When the woman told me it was free for my use as long as I lived a godly marriage, I couldn't believe my good fortune. We had a justice of the peace wedding, but I was wearing a gorgeously beautiful wedding gown. I will never forget that woman's generosity." Annabel shook her head.

"So, it made your day magical?" Gabriela asked in excitement.

Annabel laughed aloud. "Yes, it sure did. My wedding may not have been what I had imagined it to be when I was fifteen or sixteen, but it was much better than it would have been under the circumstances. Now, I have Gracen, and she's getting close to her second birthday."

"Wow! That's so amazing."

"What's your story?" Annabel leaned forward and listened as Gabriela told her about her all the financial troubles she had had. Gabriela and Annabel continued chatting until the last possible minute.

"I really need to get back to my job," Gabby said, "Or I could lose it. That is definitely not what I need right now. Look, I really enjoyed talking to you. Maybe we could get together again, and I could meet Gracen?"

"I'd like that," Annabel said. "I'll talk to you later."

Chapter 4

Gabriela finally got a reply from the other woman she had contacted about meeting: Brianne. Brianne's story had seemed really tragic, and Gabriela couldn't wait to hear about it from the woman's lips.

After the introductions, Gabriela leaned forward for Brianne's story. "I'm really glad you wanted to talk," Brianne said. "I feel like this dress has created a secret group."

"Have you ever talked to Annabel?" Gabriela asked.

"Annabel. . .Annabel. I don't think so. Was she married after me?"

"I don't remember," Gabriela said. "But I have her number. Maybe we could all three get together or even more brides."

Brianne smiled. "I like the idea. I am definitely willing to contribute. Okay, so here's what happened to me. My problem was not so much a financial one as I read in so many stories. Instead, my problem was a big fire. About five days before the date our wedding was set, some sort of electrical malfunction sparked in our house. My family lost everything. Insurance took care of the problem financially, but the dress I had so carefully picked out months before along with my shoes and veil had been consumed by the fire. Trying to get a dress five days before a wedding is pretty much impossible.

"But, this beautiful old lady performed a miracle. She let me borrow the dress. It was much better than the dress I had originally picked. Better than that, it was ready for the wedding two days early." Brianne shook her head. "I had thought I might need to call off the wedding. I was freaking out. I couldn't even go to work I was so stressed out. I had a few burn marks from escaping the house, but the dress covered them nicely. They can't even be seen in the photos."

"Wow!" Gabby said, soaking in her new friend's story. "Wow." She was silent for a few minutes as Brianne's story sunk in. "Did you know that there have been thirty-three weddings in that dress? I'll be number thirty-four."

"When is your wedding?" Brianne asked.

"It'll be mid-August, right after my sister moves into her college dorm. She's been living with me."

"Would you mind if I rudely invited myself to your wedding?" Brianne smiled.

Gabby laughed. "Of course not. You are welcome. It's going to be a small wedding, and we ask that each guest bring a dish of food, a sort of potluck. We really don't have the money for much more, but I would be honored for you to come."

After meeting the two brides, Gabby wanted to meet more. She kept setting up even more appointments with brides. She had one last meeting planned before her wedding. This meeting took a few weeks to set up. By the time Gabby met her, it was the first day of August.

"What's your story?" Gabby asked impatiently. The question had become one of which she could not wait to ask each new woman. Hallie had been married almost ten years ago.

"My story's probably a bit different from some others," Hallie shook her head. Gabby had agreed to come to her house because Hallie had three young children. Hallie wanted them to be able to play and stay out of their hair while the two women talked. "I was poor. I couldn't buy a wedding dress. That much is as normal as for any of us women."

Gabby nodded, anticipating more.

"My story becomes interesting after I married Mark. Did the lady have you make a promise?"

Gabby nodded. "Yes, I promised that I would live my marriage according to God's will."

Hallie accepted Gabby's words. "Yes, I promised the same thing. At the time, I promised it because it seemed such an easy exchange for the dress. But it wasn't as easy as I thought it would be. The first year of marriage was so difficult. I looked back on the innocence I sported on my wedding day, and I would shake my head. How had I thought I loved Mark?" Hallie was quiet as she remembered. "I was sure that we were going to get a divorce. You see, his family lives on the other side of the country. I know he was really close to them, but he agreed that living here would be the best solution for us.

"But, it was like he had forgotten that. We argued almost every night. I started to hate him. He made me cry so much." Hallie shook her head, and Gabby should see the tears brimming in her eyes. "I started fantasizing about running away and going a place where he wouldn't find me. Then, I remembered my promise. I tried to weasel my way out of it, saying that the fighting was Mark's fault. I blamed him, but I knew I needed to take credit for my part. So, I started serving Mark instead of myself.

"Even when I was tired, I would make dinner. I would clean up without complaint. He noticed after a month, and I felt him become more tender toward me. We were finally able to talk through what had been happening. That was the best day of my life, the day that we finally talked it all through without screaming. I finally slept next to him and felt connected to him again.

"Gabby, that promise is going to be hard to keep. You will probably get angry with your fiance sometimes, but don't walk away. The weak walk away; it's the strong that keep fighting."

Gabby hugged Hallie as a few tears spilled over. "Thank you, Hallie. I needed to hear those words. They were just what I needed." Before Gabby left Hallie's house, she invited her to her wedding. "I know it is only two weeks, but if you think you can come, I would really like it. Don't be shy about bringing your husband and children."

Chapter 5

On the day of her wedding, Gabby carefully donned the dress. It was to be a simple ceremony. Only her sister would stand beside her. Bryan was having his best friend stand beside him. At that moment nothing felt simple about Gabby as she waited for Reese to calmly do up the back.

"I can't believe it's really the day," Gabby said.

Reese smiled. "Yeah, I'm pretty sure I'm having the most exciting first weekend home from college out of all of my friends." Of course, her statement made Gabby start asking about all of Reese's new friends. She had to make sure that her baby sister was doing well and having fun in college.

"Is it done?" Gabby asked.

Reese nodded. "It's done. You're all ready."

"Well, not completely," Gabby said. "I look fine, but I feel a bit nervous about walking down that aisle."

"Why?" Reese asked. "Are you unsure about Bryan?"

"No," Gabby shook her head. "I know he is perfect for me, well, as perfect a fit as someone can be with my rather strange personality."

Reese laughed. "Then, what is making you nervous?"

"I guess it just hit me that this is a lifelong commitment. I love Bryan, and I just don't want anything to go wrong. What if we start living together, and he does annoying things that get on my nerves?"

"Like what?"

"Like leave his socks on the bed."

"Then tell him to take his socks off," Reese shrugged. "It's not that hard. Look, if you love him and you know that for sure, then you just have to go through the bad stuff and remember that. Then you'll get to the good times, and it'll be all worth it."

"Alright, my sister the wise," Gabby smiled. "What time is it?"

Reese looked at her phone. "We still have thirty minutes."

"What a long thirty minutes that'll be!" Gabby sighed, carefully sitting in her dress.

Reese laughed aloud. "I thought you just said you were nervous to do it, and now you can't wait to go down the aisle."

Gabriela laughed with her sister. "When you get to this point, I will be right by your side and remind you of everything you just said. Meanwhile, you'll just be like. No, I'm nervous! Let me be nervous by myself!"

Gabriela's friend Erica burst into the bedroom just then. "Hey! Wow, Gabby! You look so amazing!" Erica was the unofficial photographer. She had a professional camera and had done some photo shoots. A free photographer was her wedding gift to her friend. "Look, we don't have a lot of time, but I wanted to get a few pictures of just you in all your bridal beauty, then maybe a few with Reese. Hey, Reese! How are you?" Erica said in one breath.

Gabby laughed. "Oh, Erica, I knew there was a good reason we were friends." Erica took all the photos she wanted with Gabby sitting, standing, lounging, smiling, and serious.

"Alright, Reese, get in there with your sister." After a few more shots, Erica hovered over to the door. "Alright, I believe we have five minutes before your little flower girl will start her march. Let's get you safely down these stairs."

Gabby carefully maneuvered the stairs with the help of her sister and friend. The stairs were not very wide and definitely not prepared to have brides tramping up and down them. She finally stood by the back doors.

"Ready?" Reese asked.

Because Gabby had decided against having their estranged father walking her down the aisle, Reese would be walking right beside her.

"I think so," Gabby answered. "But ask me again in a minute, and I might have a different answer."

"You've got this, Sis."

"Thanks."

Erica reappeared as the music started to assist the flower girl on her way. Next went the ringbearer. After that came Gabby and Reese. It was a simple, small wedding, just as Gabby had dreamed it. Best of all was Bryan's face when she came through the doors of the back of the farmhouse.

His smile was genuine and delighted, and Gabby looked only at him as Reese guided her steps down the aisle. When she reached the altar, she placed her hands in Bryan's, smiling into his eyes and wondering how she had ever doubted her decision to marry him.

"I love you," she whispered as the pastor was talking to them. He mouthed the words back and gave her hands a squeeze. Suddenly, the ceremony, including a candle lighting, a song sung by a friend, and a short talk from the pastor seemed all too long to Gabby. After what seemed an eternity, the words she had wanted to hear for so long pierced her thoughts.

"You may now kiss the bride."

Gabby kissed Bryan, leaning into his lips. When they pulled back, Gabby felt the magic of the moment lingering. "You're my husband," she whispered, incredulous.

"And you, my dear, are my wife." Bryan let go of one of her hands, facing the audience. The pastor announced them, and Bryan paused before they started down the aisle. "This is my wife!" he shouted, his pleasure clear as he lifted up their joined hands in victory. Gabby started laughing. Suddenly, a huge cheer rose up from the back of the rows of seats. Gabby looked over and counted five of the former brides that she had met.

"Yes, Gabriela!" They screamed together. While Gabby had not pictured her wedding as loud as a ballgame, she couldn't help laughing aloud.

Bryan carefully led her down the steps, and they entered the old farmhouse. As soon as they were inside, Bryan turned to her and kissed her passionately. "You are the most beautiful bride I have ever seen," he whispered. "And tonight, I will make you mine." Gabby trembled with anticipation, leaning in for another kiss.

A week later, Gabby carefully zipped the wedding dress into the garment bag for the last time. She took out the book and carefully glued in a photo of herself wearing the dress. She smiled at the photo then took up a pen and began writing in her best cursive beside the photo.

"Gabriela Winfox, age twenty-five. Married to Bryan Davis on August 21, 2016. This dress changed my life. Not only did it give me a chance to have the kind of wedding I would never have had on my budget, but it showed me the friendliness and generosity this kind of world doesn't see very often. It made me promise to be a more generous person and to look for opportunities to help others. I didn't have any money for a nice wedding, and my fiance and I feared we would not be able to throw a wedding. Determined to get married, because we knew it was right, I thought I would never have a wedding dress. I was wrong. Please, contact me. I would love to talk to you, and I know that the brides I met would love to talk to you as well. We are in this together."

Gabriela signed her name under her words and closed the book with a solemn thud. "Thank you, God," she said as she loaded the dress, veil, and book into the back of her car. She was on her way to the flea market.

www.ingramcontent.com/pod-product-compliance
Lightning Source LLC
Chambersburg PA
CBHW021755150726
47989CB00004B/1669